“J. Bradley must know how to wield a sword. His sword skills extend to his prose style in BODIES MADE OF SMOKE. Each section is a critical strike, flaying the story of unnecessary skin left in many other books. The reader gets to the blood and guts of the story, which is full of blood and guts and gods and sex and of course *Highlander*.”

— Chad Redden author of THURSDAY

“A trip of time, the echoing shouts of Freddie Mercury, and papier-mâché heads clamoring under a bed. J. Bradley has conjured up an offering and built the temple from pages. The temple hides no folly proclaiming that death is near; it's unavoidable, even the immortals tremble as it passes by. Bradley's words are the quivers in an earthquake. Yes this is destruction, but it's equally a rebirth.”

— Matt DeBenedictis, author of CONGRATULATIONS! THERE'S NO LAST PLACE IF EVERYONE IS DEAD

“BODIES MADE OF SMOKE is at once a story of true detection, a critical analysis of the cult film *Highlander*, a *New York Times* best-selling guide to more frequent one-night-stands; all my new favorite things. Step back, this novella swings. There is only one. J. Bradley stuns with this sexy new work.”

— Jason Teal, editor, HEAVY FEATHER REVIEW

BODIES MADE OF SMOKE

a novella
by

J. BRADLEY

HOUSEFIRE
www.housefirebooks.com

ISBN: 978-1-937395-02-5

Cover design by L. Ruoff and Robert Duncan Gray

Interior layout by L. Ruoff

Edited by L. Ruoff and Riley Michael Parker

Printed in the United States of America.

To my mom.
Thanks for not murdering me after all these years.

CONTENTS

BODIES MADE OF SMOKE

1

I.

'With enough Clan MacGregor in me, I'm all fuckin' Highlander. That's right baby, and I know that ass ain't hallowed, so tonight there can be only one in that ass. There can be only one.'

Mario keeps watching Sarah on the screen as she tries to figure out where the voice came from, her back kneading the wall.

'Who the fuck are you? Who. The fuck. Are you?' Sarah yells.

'I am immortal and soon you'll have the blood of kings swimmin' in your tubes.'

Mario hears the cut of Sarah's scream as the screen blackens through the filter of his fingers.

II.

The TV screen flickers.

'I am immortal. I have inside me the blood of kings.'

"Sarah playing 'Princes of the Universe' on repeat was almost a deal-breaker—until she said it was only for fucking. She loved it when I timed my *YEAH!*s with Freddie Mercury's. It took about a week to memorize the dialogue:

'Who has no rival?'

'No one, baby, no one.'

'Who has no equal?'

'No one, baby, no one.'

'Who's the ruler of your universe?'

'You are. You. Are. Youuuuuuooohhh…'

Always after the third question, the tower of her flopped on the other side of the bed. Her left hand reached for the stereo remote and slapped Freddie's mouth shut."

"Why did you stay with her?"

"Well, there's a law of averages where *x* is based on hotness and fuck skills and *y* is how fucking crazy they are. If *x* exceeds *y*, then stick with them. If *y* exceeds *x*, get out, and for a while, I never wondered about Sarah's fetish because she fucked like a power chord. Shit, when I broke the CD in front of her as my way of saying fuck you and goodbye, she just pulled out another one and popped it into the stereo. I heard her yell 'There can only be one!' through the door as I slammed it in her face … You found my name and number where?"

"Inside the neck stump of a papier-mâché sculpture of your face. It was under her bed."

III.

In this scene, John Landis Mason slow dances with Hephaestus at a generic homecoming dance. Hephaestus cinches Mason's hips, pulls him a little closer as Gary Cherone sings "More Than Words." Before their mouths meet, Mason wakes up in a cold sweat. He rushes to his drafting table and sketches what will become the machine that makes the lid that gives jars Mason's surname.

In this scene, Tom grabs a fistful of ice from the freezer and throws it into a questionably clean Mason jar. He takes a half-filled bottle of Clan MacGregor from the open pantry and pours it into the jar until it is three-quarters full. Tom opens the bottle of Chek Cola on the counter and adds an aftertaste. In four swallows, Tom slays the cocktail. He slurs before collapsing in the kitchen.

In this scene, Mario moves the Mason jar around the room like a net. He seals it tight. Mario grabs another Mason jar and lid from the box in the corner. He moves the fresh Mason jar around the room like a net. He seals it tight. Mario grabs another Mason jar and lid from the box in the corner. He thinks of Sarah as he moves the jar around the room, again, like a net. He seals it tight.

In this scene, Hephaestus watches over Mason's shoulders like a proud parent as the machine that will eventually make the lid that gives jars Mason's surname takes shape.

IV.

Poem found in Sarah's nightstand:

Duncan MacLeod Drinks Alone

Your vagina is like the blade of a katana.
You make it hot like a sauna.
When we hump, I want to be your neck stump.
Like a moth to the flame, let me be the blame
for the shame and the stains.

Take off your pants, let me see those moons
wax and wain on the plane of my face.
It's such a disgrace that this night will end soon,
that I won't get to wake up next to you again
and count the ways to make you swoon.

Written on the bottom:

While I appreciate your clever use of internal rhyme, this is more of an erotic poem than a love poem, which is not the purpose of this workshop. I like where you're going, but see if you can bring it down from X to PG-13. I'm confident you can.

V.

"Sarah was just like anyone else. She paid her $20 and did the session. It's not my place to judge the content or her objectives. I just teach people how to write love poems."

"Do you remember her contribution to the class?"

"Do I remember that poem? Yeah, I do. I've never met someone with such a *Highlander* fetish before. She brought in that song from the *Highlander* movies as her favorite love poem. Again, not my place to judge, but it was weird."

VI.

"I want to blacken out the facts like eyes," Mario says into the open Mason jar before sealing it tight and placing it in the box with all the other sealed Mason jars.

VII.

Hephaestus leans against the armoire, stretching Mason's plans out to see all the details. He adds a couple of extra pieces here and there before putting it back on Mason's drafting board. Hephaestus unfreezes time, lights his pipe. The smoke telegraphs that all is going according to plan.

VIII.

August 2nd

My favorite episode of *Highlander: The Series* is where Tessa gets killed and then they play “Who Wants to Live Forever” as Duncan holds her in his arms. That’s the way I want to be married—like I’m dying and that song playing as he kisses me for the first time. Who wants to live forever when love must die?

IX.

"Daddy, I don't want to go to sleep. That man's voice is just gonna be in my ear saying mean things all night."

"Sarah, there's no man in your head. You sneak over to the TV and turn it on an hour after I put you to bed. That's what you're hearing."

"Daddy, no. He comes out of my ear as a cloud and flips the TV on before going back in my ear."

"You have such a wild imagination. Now go to bed."

X.

The fingers go first, becoming translucent, then wisps, the wind casting them into the clouds. The wrists, forearms, upper arms, shoulders follow before the legs go. The entire time a god disappears, you watch the spectrum of emotions in the face, which is the last thing that fades away into the atmosphere.

XI.

"Daddy, what are you doing in my apartment?"

Mario looks up from the veil of his hands and sees Sarah standing in the doorway of her bedroom. "Sarah? I thought you were kidnapped or worse."

"What do you mean?"

"I watched the tape Tom mailed me. Then I showed your landlord what was on it and he let me into your apartment to try to find out what was going on. I called first, but your cell phone was out of service. I was worried."

"God damn it, why the fuck did Tom send that to you? That fuck. Where's the tape?" Mario takes it out of the box filled with sealed Mason jars and hands it to Sarah.

"Is everything OK, Sarah?"

"Yeah, Daddy, why do you ask?"

Mario shakes his head for a moment before picking up the box of Mason jars. "Now that I know you're OK, I guess I'll get going."

XII.

Sarah walks into the closet and pulls the chain attached to the light. The back wall slides down, revealing a hidden room. She walks through the opening and the wall behind her slides back up. In front of Sarah is a large tank resembling a sealed Mason jar. Sarah places her left index finger and thumb around her right wrist and twists counterclockwise. Her clothing and skin fold into a bracelet, leaving Hephaestus in her place. He presses a switch on the bracelet and it teleports from his hand into the sealed Mason jar. The bracelet unpacks to show Sarah, fully dressed and unconscious. Hephaestus leans against the jar, the sweat from his brow dripping into his beard.

I only had about five minutes of blood left before the body would have collapsed and I would have been exposed.

Hephaestus grabs the cane leaning against the Mason jar and walks to a console. He punches a few buttons and watches the papier-mâché heads stare at Mario, Mason jars as nets, frantic phone calls.

What video is Sarah talking about? How was she able to keep that from me?

XIII.

Tom peers at the space beneath the closed pantry door, his chin sore from hitting the linoleum. His elbows ache as he pushes himself into a kneeling position, his right hand gripping the refrigerator handle. Tom tries rubbing swarms from his temples, smacking the cotton moths out of his mouth. He almost buckles, but wisps of sobriety keep his kneecaps intact. Tom grabs a bottle of open beer from the fridge, takes a sip, and puts the bottle back. He starts wiping his mouth on his coat sleeve and notices, quarter-wipe, that he's wearing a coat. Tom looks down and sees jeans on his legs, a blood spot on the right toe of his black Converse shoe. He reopens the refrigerator and sees the open bottle of beer, unidentified take out boxes, an eighth of butter, Mrs. Butterworth in need of a transfusion. Tom shuts the refrigerator, slowly walks out of the kitchen, and looks around. An empty pizza box sits on the dining room table, open and starving. Yesterday's outfit lounges on the couch. The double-doors to the washer and dryer are still open, clothing hanging out of the dryer like torn-out arteries.

Tom flips the light switch in the hall, walks slowly while looking at the walls. The paint chips and nicks look all the same. He opens the bathroom door, turns on the light, studies the smudges on the mirror, the loose facial hair in and around the sink, the hard water bleeding from the tile in the shower. Tom rubs his head for a moment before walking out of the bathroom and closing the door.

Tom walks into the bedroom, slipping out of the shoes, peeling off the jacket and jeans. He flops face down onto the bed and then, rolling onto his back, sees

ATROPOS LIVES

written on the wall in blood. A severed head on the dresser stares at Tom with its blue eyes, black goatee, hair pulled back in a ponytail.

XIV.

Atropos snaps her shears and hands them to the blacksmith. “Hurry. We don’t have much time.”

XV.

What are they doing here? Hephaestus says to himself while watching two men knocking at Sarah's door on the monitors. They look like extras in an episode of *Law & Order*. Hephaestus points to the Mason jar and Sarah folds into a bracelet, then appears in his hand. He puts the bracelet on his right wrist, twists it clockwise. Sarah walks out of the secret room and answers the door, the chain on.

"How can I help you?"

"Are you Sarah Brent?" The one on the left says, peering above his horn-rimmed glasses.

"I am. And you are?" She has badges for eyes.

"I'm Detective John Fresno. This is Detective Aaron Sisco. We have some questions about this man. Maybe you can answer them for us." Sisco pulls out of his pocket a Polaroid of a man with blue eyes, a goatee, hair pulled back.

2

I.

“Vulcan, darling, it is time to wake up.”

“Aphrodite, there better not be someone in bed with us.”

“Who’s Aphrodite? Another one of your consorts?”

Hephaestus turns over to look at the woman lying next to him. “Aphrodite, quit playing games with me.”

“Vulcan, I’m not playing games. I’m your wife, Venus. Did you sneak out to have drinks with Bacchus last night?”

Hephaestus gets out of bed, throws on clothes. He leans against a wall, his forehead resting on his forearm. “I’m sorry, Venus. I had a dream that your name was Aphrodite and mine was Hephaestus. We were watching the people of Greece and laughing at how silly mortals are sometimes.”

Venus wraps her arms around Hephaestus’s waist and kisses his neck. “It’s OK, my husband. You can stay here while I go see what offerings were left at my temple.”

II.

Detective Fresno walks around Sarah's apartment, noticing the *Highlander* movie posters and autographed photos of Christopher Lambert and Adrian Paul all over the walls. He motions to Sisco, and the two sit across from Sarah, Fresno with a notepad open.

"Ms. Brent, how do you know Michael Venti?"

"Mike and I were lovers for a short period of time."

"How did you two break up?"

"He walked out on me and I was OK with that. He wasn't the one I always wanted anyway. We haven't talked since."

Sisco leans forward, placing his elbows on his knees.

"Ms. Brent, he was found beheaded. We're still looking for the head. Did Michael have any enemies you were aware of?" Sarah covers her mouth with her hand, shakes her head. Sisco leans forward and hands Sarah a business card. "This is my number. If you know anything, call me, please. Thank you for your time, Ms. Brent." Sisco turns toward the door. "Fresno, let's go."

After the door shuts, Sarah locks it and puts the chain on. She walks into her bedroom, reaches under her bed and slowly pulls out a laminated poster of *Highlander II: The Quickening* with papier-mâché heads on top of it, positioned to stare into each other's eyes. She picks up Michael's head, slides the rest back underneath her bed, and takes it into the kitchen.

Hello, Hephaestus.

"Who is that?"

You know who I am, Hephaestus.

"Why do you keep calling me Hephaestus?"

That is to whom I am speaking. You can ignore me all you want, Hephaestus. I know where you are now and I am coming for you.

"Atropos, I have escaped you before and I will escape you again as I always do."

No one can escape death. Not even you, Hephaestus. Not even you.

Sarah places Michael's papier-mâché head in the sink and sets it on fire. The flames eat the scalp, his "o" face. She takes baking soda out of the refrigerator and pours it onto the fire, then reaches into the drawer next to the sink for tongs and pushes the remains into the garbage disposal.

III.

"Sarah? This is a surprise. Would you like to come in?" Nate looks her up and down: trench coat, pony tail, fuck-me heels. Sarah walks into the apartment like smoke, reclines in the brown leather chaise lounge. She parts her legs slightly, revealing her tan, athletic calves. "Is there something I can help you with?"

Sarah crooks her finger. Nate climbs on top of her, sliding his hand up her thigh, kissing her neck.

"Mmmmm, baby?"

"Yes, Sarah?"

"There can be only one."

Nate's head lands on the living room table. Sarah wipes her sword on the trench coat before hiding it inside. She picks up Nate's head and walks out of his apartment. The camera catches the warpaint of his blood on her face, the trophy dangling from her clenched hand.

IV.

Hephaestus brings down the hammer on a round piece of metal held against the anvil with his tongs. *My name is Hephaestus. My name is Hephaestus. My name is Hephaestus.* He wills the metal to finish cooling and then picks up the bracelet. *Simple, but should do the trick. Now, to find a worthy bearer.*

V.

"We got the bitch, Fresno. All there on video tape. The blood, that head. Let's get the arrest warrant now."

VI.

Sarah walks into the apartment. The head stopped dripping blood four blocks back. She looks into the mirror and sees a man's face instead of her own.

You've done well, Tom. Quite well. Put the head with the other in the bedroom and then have a drink. We will have Hephaestus flushed out soon.

VII.

"Mortal, how did you get into our home?" Venus yells at the fully armored Roman centurion. "Best answer quick or else I will punish you." The fully armored Roman centurion twists his right wrist counterclockwise. The armor, skin, collapses into a bracelet.

"Hello darling."

"Vulcan, why would you play such a nasty trick?"

"It's not a nasty trick. It's how I will survive when Rome burns. It's how you can survive if you want."

"Rome burning? Under our protection? Hardly. What madness plagues you?"

"When Rome doesn't exist any more, neither will we. We are only as powerful as the belief poured into us. The Greeks gave us shape. The Romans changed our names."

"You are a fool, Vulcan. Man did not give us shape, we gave man his shape."

"My name is Hephaestus. Hephaestus. Hephaestus. You are Aphrodite. Don't you remember?" Venus shakes her head sorrowfully.

"Vulcan … my husband, why are you so troubled? Why do you keep calling me Aphrodite? Has Juno done something wicked to you to punish me for my infidelity with Mars? I don't know how many times I have to apologize."

"Aphrodite, I love you. I will always love you. I'm sorry you won't let me save you." Hephaestus presses the bracelet in two different places and puts his hand on Venus's forehead. "Venus, I am going on a quest to find the most precious of metals to make you a beautiful necklace. That's what you'll remember when you are asked where I am. Now sleep."

Hephaestus catches Aphrodite in his arms, puts her into their bed. He looks at her one last time before turning the bracelet clockwise, walking out of his home as a Roman centurion.

VIII.

"Atropos, why have you tasked me to do this?"

"Do you dare question a god, especially one who can cut your thread earlier than planned?" The blacksmith shakes his head. "Good. You must melt my shears and cast them with iron into the mold of a Xiphos. You have three nights to complete the blade. I will return at that time to claim it."

IX.

Mario opens one of the Mason jars, smells it. He coughs up volcanic ash, charred flesh. He opens another Mason jar, smells it. He can't get the taste of Pompeii out of his throat. Mario opens another Mason jar, smells it. He feels mushroom clouds in the back of his eyes. Mario's right breast vibrates. He pulls the cell phone out of his pocket and answers.

"Mario, did you find the heads?" Mario moves the cell phone away from his face, stares at the number in the display, before putting it back onto his ear.

"I did. What sick games are you two into, Tom?"

"The *Highlander* rape games, the video taping—all her idea. I didn't know about the heads beneath the bed until one day when she left me at her place while she went to the store. I'm sorry I had to send you one of our sessions, but it was the only way I could get you to believe me."

"Tom, I think something is really wrong with her. I took some samples of the air using my Mason jars ..."

"What? Mason jars?"

"Hear me out, Tom. They help catch the color and shape of Sarah's moods. I've done it ever since she was little and started complaining about a man's voice in her head. I've never smelled anything like this before, burning skin, charred buildings."

"Mario, I think what you're smelling is probably drugs. Maybe meth and pot mixed together."

"No no no, that's not possible, Sarah would never do drugs."

"She has papier-mâché heads of all of her exes under her bed, Mario, and all of their faces look like they were cumming in, or around, or near her. Snap fucking out of it. We need to have an intervention before she does something stupid."

Mario sighs, "You're right. She's sick. She needs help. When?"

"Tonight. Meet me at her place at 8:00 PM. She should be home by then."

"OK. And thank you for being so good to my daughter."

"See you in a few hours." Tom hangs up the cell phone, places it on the counter near the stove. He raises the sword in his right hand to the ceiling. *It's time for us to rest, Tom. Tonight, we finish this game.* The blade disappears into the back of Tom's neck, his skin swallowing the hilt as he collapses to the floor.

X.

John, your body is dying. There's not much time left.

"What do I do, Hephaestus?"

I need you to twist your wrist counterclockwise.

Mason twists his wrist counterclockwise. A bronze bracelet appears.

Slide the bracelet off, put it into a Mason jar. Seal the lid tight.

"I thought you needed a new body right away or else you would—"

The sealed jar will protect me until someone finds me again. Someone always does.

"Will we still be able to talk?"

Once you seal me away, you will hear my voice no more. You're the first mortal in thousands of years that I have enjoyed being a part of. You would have been a worthy servant in my time. Goodbye, John.

"Goodbye, Hephaestus." The bronze bracelet clinks into the bottom of the Mason jar. Mason seals it tight.

XI.

"Daddy, look what I found." Sarah unscrews the Mason jar and pulls out the bronze bracelet at the bottom. She puts it on her right wrist. "Doesn't it look pretty, Daddy?"

Mario kneels down and looks Sarah in the eyes. "It looks old and dangerous. You need to give that to me, right now young lady." Sarah presses a couple of hidden studs on the bracelet and puts her hand on Mario's head.

"This bracelet was never found. There was never any bracelet. You will remember nothing and you will never wonder why. When we go to the couch, you will awake. Do you understand?" Mario nods. "Good, Daddy. Let's go watch cartoons."

XII.

What are those two cops doing back here? Hephaestus watches Sisco and Fresno pacing nervously outside the door through his surveillance array. He zooms in and sees a folded piece of paper in Sisco's hand. *Damn it. I better get rid of them before they search this place.*

Hephaestus lets Sarah's skin and clothes wrap around him as she walks out of the secret room to the front door. She unlocks it and begins to open the door cautiously, when a body forces its way through. Sarah is thrown back, the open door revealing Tom standing in the threshold. She looks behind her to see the body skid across the hardwood floor and collide with the couch in the living room. The body, her father, lay unconscious. When Sarah turns to look at Tom again, he's clutching a sword in his right hand.

"Tom, what are you doing with that sword?"

"Stop being coy, Hephaestus. I've spent thousands of years chasing you. Time for us to join our brothers and sisters once and for all. Turn on the TV."

On the TV Sarah sees herself covered in blood, holding Nate's head.

3

I.

James Decatur, professional wingman, watches his client, Tom, teaspoon-nurse a Pabst tallboy and eye the women chatting at the bar.

"See anything you like?" James asks when "Paradise City" fades into "Rio." Tom nods his head. "Which one?" He raises his eyebrows and tips his head toward the blonde at the bar wearing a black and yellow polka dot dress, black flats, no visible tats. "Classy but attainable. What's your opening gonna be?"

"I'm just gonna go up and say how much I like that dress of hers and then introduce myself."

"That's the fastest way to make yourself a character in one of those shitty Kate Hudson movies where you're the cockblocked friend trying to floss her between your foreskin. Here's what you're going to do: you are going to go to the bar and order a drink and subtly overhear what she is talking about with her friends. Then you'll use a loose thread of that conversation to make your way in. Understood?" Tom nods. "Do you have your Bluetooth headset?" Tom nods again. "Good, turn it on. I'm calling your phone. Leave it on in your pocket so I can hear you and text you if necessary. Good luck."

II.

"Blacksmith, have you done what I've asked?"

"I have, Atropos."

"Good. Hand me the blade." The blacksmith hands the Xiphos to Atropos. She holds it up in the light of the forge, inspecting the edge with her thumb. "Blacksmith, I am going to ask you to perform a task and you will have the choice to accept or refuse."

"What if I refuse?"

"I will test the effectiveness of your creation on you."

"Not much of a choice is there?"

"There is always a choice, Blacksmith."

"What is this task you will ask of me, Threadcutter?"

"To keep your creation safe until it is needed. I will ensure your bloodline is blessed for as long as this is done. Do we have a deal?"

"We have a deal, Atropos." The blacksmith shakes Atropos's bony, frail hand. She twists the blacksmith's arm until he kneels, his back facing Atropos. She takes the Xiphos, cuts the arm holding the blacksmith down, dipping the tip in the wound. "What are you doing?"

"Getting the weapon ready for safekeeping. Keep your head down, Blacksmith." Atropos raises the Xiphos high before plunging it into the base of the blacksmith's neck. He howls as the blade sinks, his skin swallowing the hilt. Atropos releases the blacksmith from the hold, allowing him to collapse onto the floor.

"What did you do, Atropos?" The blacksmith rolls around on his back, sucking in large amounts of air between every word.

"The answer to your question is inside you. Search within. Farewell, Blacksmith. We will not meet again."

III.

"James, can you still hear me?"

"Yeah. What's going on, Tom?"

"I'm waiting for that girl you helped me pick up to come out of the bathroom. She's got *Highlander* shit all over the living room, man."

"That's a little weird. Is that a dealbreaker for you?"

"No. Strangely, it isn't. I haven't ever felt this way about a girl. She makes my back tingle. I think she might be the one."

"Slow down, Tom. Nothing turns a woman off faster than love at first sight. It only works if she's twelve. You need to keep that shit to yourself, you understand?"

"I understand. How can I ever thank you, man?"

"The check clearing without a problem is all the thanks I'll need. See you tomorrow for the pick up."

IV.

"Atropos, what have you done?"

"Cornered you, Hephaestus. Even if you escape from me, you won't escape from the authorities. I will get to you—today, tomorrow, eventually."

Sarah passes her left hand over her right wrist revealing a bronze bracelet. Tom nicks his arm, lets a drop of blood spill onto the floor. The clock in the living room stops.

"This duel will end when one of us draws our final breath, or when the mortal wakes up." Tom points at Mario's unconscious body. "But he will be out for a very, very long time. Ready yourself, Hephaestus."

Sarah touches the bronze bracelet with her left hand, brushing forward, then backward. The bronze bracelet reveals a large, double-edged blade just above the hand. The bottom of the bracelet expands, covering the forearm. "I am ready for you now, Atropos."

V.

"Jesus Christ. What happened here?"

"Well Detective Fresno, his head is missing, her stomach and throat have crooked grins, and this guy is belly-paddling in his own blood, holding onto this sword, which looks like the murder weapon."

"What the hell is this?" Fresno bends down to retrieve something from the floor.

"For fuck sake, don't you know how to use gloves?"

"Sisco, it's a piece of bronze. *Antiques Roadshow* shit, man. I bet this is worth a lot."

"There's another piece over there. Take a look."

"Pieced together, it's … some sort of bracelet. It looks like it was cut in half, not by the sword though, because the cut looks like it comes from above and below."

"So what the hell cut it?"

"Good question, Sisco. Wait—did you hear that?"

"The belly-paddler? That's just gotta be air comin' out from him."

"Yeah." Fresno places a pocket mirror under the man's nostrils. "Holy shit, he's still breathing."

"I'll call for a cart. We might find out what happened here just yet."

VI.

"You know, no one's ever wanted to slow dance with me to this song," Sarah sighs into Tom's shoulder between Freddie Mercury's rising vocals. "I could live forever like this, Tom."

"Yeah? I'm feeling that way about you, too." Tom connects his hands on the small of Sarah's back, pulls her closer until he feels her heart beat against his. He moves his hand to cup Sarah's chin, lifting her head up, and kisses her slowly as Freddie Mercury asks, "Who wants to live forever?" Their lips part with the end of the question, and Sarah rests against Tom's chest.

"Is there a place for us? Is there time for us?"

"Yeah, baby. Yeah there is. We'll make sure there is."

VII.

"Alexios, why did Atropos see you?" Hephaestus stands outside of the blacksmith's shop.

"She asked me to keep something safe for her."

"You best not be lying to me, Alexios." Hephaestus closes the distance. "You know what I could do to you."

"And you know what I could do to you if you touch him." The smoke coming from the hearth forms into an old, frail woman standing between Alexios and Hephaestus. "This man is going to make sure we meet our final fate. Even gods must die eventually."

VIII.

That woman is not a woman. A god is using her like a meat puppet.

"I don't believe you."

You have a job to do, boy, as every male in your bloodline has had this job to do. It's how your family has survived for generations.

"I don't want to do it. I'm in love with her. You can't ask me to do this."

I don't have to ask.

Tom's legs move his body into the kitchen. His hand grabs a fistful of ice from the freezer and throws it into a questionably clean Mason jar, then takes a half-filled bottle of Clan MacGregor from the open pantry and pours it into the jar until it is three-quarters full. His hand opens the bottle of Chek Cola on the counter and adds an aftertaste. His arm raises the glass to his open lips, and in four swallows, the jar is empty. The cocktail pulses through his veins. "Whhhhhyyyyyy," he slurs before collapsing.

A moment later Tom picks himself up. He bends his head down, reaches behind his neck. With a curdling scream, he pulls the Xiphos out of the sheath of his spine, brandishes it so Atropos can see herself in the blade.

"Because we have a job to do."

IX.

"Uhhhhh what happened?" Mario comes to, rubbing his head. He sees Sarah wearing a gauntlet with a blade parrying Tom's sword. Mario pushes himself up to his knees. "What … are you two … doing?"

"Atropos, the mortal is awake. Our duel is finished—for now."

"Not this time, Hephaestus." In a flash, Tom runs Mario through with his sword.

"Why, Tom?"

"For the greater good." Tom pulls the blade out of Mario's gut. Mario's head sits neatly against the back of his feet. Sarah tries running to her bedroom but is pushed back into the living room.

"The seal didn't break?"

"No, Hephaestus, it didn't. The mortal wasn't completely conscious and aware of his surroundings. I learned that from our duel during the Seven Years War." Tom cleans the sword with his shirt. "Shall we continue?"

X.

"Daddy, why won't you do anything about the man that talks to me every night?"

"What man? I keep telling you, you're leaving the TV on when you fall asleep. I think I'll just take it out of your room."

Sarah, quit lying to your father.

Sarah watches her left hand touch the bronze bracelet.

"Daddy, I'm sorry. You're right. Would you kiss me goodnight?" As Mario leans down, Sarah touches his temple. "You will not remember this conversation. You will leave the TV in the room. You will always leave the TV in the room. Now kiss me goodnight and turn on the TV. *Highlander: The Series* is going to be on in a few minutes." Mario kisses Sarah goodnight and turns on the TV before closing the bedroom door. He can't hear Sarah scream.

XI.

"Does it mess with your sense of self to be in the body of a woman, Hephaestus? To feel her body blossom? Do you pay attention to the way her womb flutters when she sees a fresh child? Can you feel the way it teethes at you as it stays empty?

"I could ask the same of you Atropos. Always men. Why?"

"It is the pact I made with the blacksmith. He was to keep the instrument safe until called for. Each first born of the bloodline must bear the responsibility of wielding the weapon to cleanse the world of the last god."

"Why are you telling me this now?"

"Because I know where you are now, and I will have you cornered soon. Now, awake."

Sarah sits straight up in bed, her brow soaked.

"Who … is … Atropos?" she gasps.

Never mind you, girl. Sleep now.

Sarah collapses back in bed, dreaming of nothing.

XII.

Mario sneaks into Sarah's room while she sleeps, carrying a box of unopened Mason jars. He opens one, walks around the room catching the air, then seals it. He opens another one, walks around the room catching the air, then seals it. He fills all twelve of them before taking them back to the living room. Mario opens each one and inhales, trying to understand the geography of his daughter.

XIII.

An Ode to My Love, for Whom I Would Pretend to Be Immortal

Let me wrap you in my arms like a trench coat,
dig around us until we have a bottomless moat
keeping us safe and together.
                                        Whether
we watch each other break and sag, weather
wrinkles, osteoporosis, or dementia,
I want to be your only one foreva.

James lowers the cellphone, choking down his laughter. He takes a deep breath and raises it back up to his ear.

"Do you want my professional advice, Tom?"

"Yeah, I do, James. That's why I hired you."

"I think she'll love it."

4

I.

Hephaestus looks over and sees Ares standing on a rock, watching their unit fight against the foreign hordes. His eyes fix on a gleam of sunlight stretched across Ares's shield.

"With Mars on our side, we will not lose to these bastards," Hephaestus hears a distant Serveus say.

Ares drops his shield. He crouches down on the rock, clutching his stomach. The fingers become translucent, then wisps, the wind casting them into the clouds. His wrists, forearms, upper arms, and shoulders follow before the legs go.

An axe head bites into Hephaestus's shoulder. He yells out in pain as he grabs the barbarian by the arms and forces the body through his own sword. As he releases the barbarian to the ground, he slips the bracelet onto the wrist of his new host.

Soon, I'll drown in the blood and screams of Roman scum.

II.

"Dad, I'm sick of all this sword training. Why do we have to do it every day?"

"Tom, one day when you are ready, I will tell you why. Until then, until you can defeat me in combat, en garde!"

III.

"You look really good, baby." Sarah looks at Tom standing in the doorway of her bedroom, eying his clip-on pony tail and closed smoke-gray trench coat. "Are you ready to do this?"

"Not really. I'm not comfortable with this."

"I'm a consenting adult, you're a consenting adult. Come on, don't you want to make me happy?"

"I do."

"Good. Where's that bottle of Clan MacGregor I asked you to bring?" Tom pulls it out of his trench coat. "Have you been practicing your Scottish accent?" Tom nods. "Good, take a drink, and let's begin. Maybe this will be the thing that finally forces the voice out of my head. Maybe."

IV.

Tom inhales around the blade in his stomach, looking deep into Sarah's eyes. Sarah pulls the blade out, a Pollock-esque arc of blood hitting the wall. She cleans it against the couch, notices Tom still standing. "Why are you bleeding blood instead of smoke? How are you still standing?"

"Because, Hephaestus, I do not use the body as a puppet in the same way you do. You needed to see that it will not be easy to kill me." Tom raises his sword. "Shall we continue, Hephaestus?"

V.

You will not have sex with that boy.

"Why not? Afraid you might like a dick inside of you? I thought Greek men were into boy-on-boy action."

The mortals, yes, but not us. You will not have sex with that boy. Sex with a girl on the other hand . . .

"Typical boy dream, girls kissing girls. That's fucking gross. You've stopped me from many things—the fifth and eighth grade back-to-school and end-of-school dances, Homecoming last year. I am fucking this boy and you are going to deal with it. You hijacked my body, fucker, now I get to hijack you. Prepare to take it, bitch."

VI.

Alexander nicks his forearm with his sword, lets a single drop of blood fall to the floor. Tom looks at his watch and notices the face frozen at 4 and 7.

"Dad, what's going on?"

"Tom, the time has come. This duel will end when one of us draws our last breath." Alexander unsheathes the sword around his waist and throws it at Tom's feet. "Pick it up, boy. Let's see if you are worthy enough to claim your bloodright."

"I don't want to fight, Dad." Tom walks backward to the front door. Something punches his spine. He staggers toward the sword and then falls.

"I told you, boy, this duel will end when one of us draws our last breath. Pick it up. Or do you want to end up like your brother Samuel?"

VII.

It hasn't been the same since you left us, Val. There's something wrong with our daughter. I keep trying to figure it out using these Mason jars. I keep trying to bring you back, see if I can breathe in enough of your scattered atoms and have you live in me. I keep trying to shake this feeling—I'm forgetting things. I wish I could forget you sometimes. I shouldn't have said that, but I can't swallow the words sometimes. I keep saying sometimes a lot sometimes. Fuck.

What is it like when you get a letter from me? Do the words unfold from the ash and smoke? I hope to find out someday. I hope you read this.

Mario

VIII.

Tom parries Sarah's overhand blow, hard, driving her arm back and exposing her stomach. Tom lunges. Sarah twists. Sarah goes for another overhand swing. Tom parries from behind his back, turns to face her. He notices Sarah drowning in sweat, sucking and swallowing air.

"Nice … try … Atropos."

"Really? Are you sure?"

Sarah looks down and sees the small slit in her white tank top, blood, wisps of smoke seeping out. The blade shortens. She cuts a strip of her pants off, wraps it around her torso, tight. She extends her arm and the blade grows back to its original size.

"I don't think you'll have enough clothing to stop all the bleeding you're going to do, Hephaestus."

IX.

Tom parries Alexander's overhand blow, hard, driving his arm back, exposing his stomach. Tom lunges. Alexander twists. Alexander goes for another overhand swing. Tom parries from behind his back, turns to face him. He notices Alexander drowning in sweat, sucking and swallowing air.

"Nice … try … Tom."

"Are you sure about that, Dad?"

Alexander feels his stomach, notices the slit in his shirt, the drops of blood seeping out onto the floor.

"There's hope for you yet, boy. Whenever you're ready, continue."

X.

"Tom, remember, when I say 'Who. The fuck. Are you?' to set off the smoke bomb. Do you understand?" He nods, feels the remote in his trench coat pocket.

The things I do for love.

XI.

Alexander knocks Tom's sword out of his hand. Tom's foot sinks into Alexander's stomach, follows up with the crunch of a broken nose on his knee. Tom picks up his father's sword, points it at his throat.

"Youah moah ruthless than I thawght, boyah," Alexander moans through the bandage of his hands.

Finish him, Tom.

"Who said that?"

"Fimmish me, tham anahwyaquestions'llbeawnserd."

XII.

Tom notices through the slit of his eyelids the tubes coming out of his arms. He tries stretching until the steel of a handcuff bites into his left wrist.

“He’s finally awake, Fresno.”

“Whas … goin’ on?”

“You’re under arrest for the murder of Sarah and Mario Brent.”

XIII.

Sarah, what are you doing?

"Showing you the door." Sarah pushes the razor into her left wrist and slides it upward. Blood and smoke spill out of the wound into the lukewarm bathwater. She's too weak to fight her right hand from touching the side of her head.

Sarah, you will never try to kill yourself again. Now, get out of the tub, bandage that up, and then sleep. In the morning, you won't remember what has happened. You won't even see the scar.

Sarah pulls herself out of the tub, leaving a trail of blood to the sink.

XIV.

Sarah knocks the sword out of Tom's hand. Tom stands still a moment before rubbing his face and shaking his head. "Where … am … I?" Tom feels fire inside his stomach. His finger dives into the shallow water of the stab wound. Sarah lunges, the blade through Tom's right shoulder pins him to the floor.

"Where are you, Atropos? I know you're in there somewhere."

Tom, wake up. You are going to die if you don't snap out of it and get your head in the game.

"You used me like a fucking puppet, you fuck."

"Are you talking to the threadcutter? Where is she?" Sarah twists the blade, expanding the wound. Tom howls.

You weren't doing what you were supposed to do. We need to work together if we are to slay the last god. If we do it right, I can also save Sarah.

"Alright, Atropos, let's do it your way."

The blade shortens as Sarah gets closer to Tom's face. "Where is—" Tom jabs a thumb into Sarah's windpipe. While she starves for air, he kicks her stomach, knocking

Sarah and the blade out of his shoulder. Tom staggers over to his sword, picks it up.

Feeling better, Tom?

"Much better. Get up, Hephaestus." Sarah slowly makes her way to her feet. The blade on her wrist extends to its original size. "You've tormented her for too long."

"Sarah is mine to do with as I please, Tom. Oh, she found a way to keep me quiet now and again and I've always found a way around her plans. When I find the right man, I will allow him to impregnate Sarah. Once I am in the fetus, I can never, ever be killed. I will be a true god again."

Tom, he's right. A natural transfer of his essence would be permanent. He would lose his memories until the body fully matures, but once it does, Hephaestus could never truly die.

"Then we have to make sure that doesn't happen, Hephaestus. Let's finish this."

"Oh Tom, Atropos, you won't be able to kill me. I'd never lived in a body since it was a child before. I've learned some new tricks." Sarah twists the bracelet clockwise. Muscles and hair cover her arms, chest, stomach, and legs. A man's face, beard, and scalp cover her head like a helmet. A large hammer appears in his left hand. "Behold, Atropos, my true form."

"Where's Sarah?"

"Safe. For now."

"Atropos, I thought he couldn't exist like this."

"When you invoked the duel, you froze time. When you killed the mortal, you removed the only witness. There's no disbelief here that could hurt me."

He's right, Tom. We've created a pocket universe Hephaestus can exist in without consequence.

"Have you ever fought him when he's at full strength?"

No.

Hephaestus rushes, swings his hammer overhead. Tom parries. The blow traps his sword between the hammer head and the floor. Hephaestus's giant left hand sends Tom flying into the adjacent wall.

"I have you now, Threadcutter. How much more can the mortal shell that you hide in take?"

Tom, how are you?

"My face feels like a truck crushed it."

I'll block the pain. We need to finish this quickly or else he'll put you in a state even I can't fix.

"How?"

I can sense Sarah's life energy powering his true form. He knows he has to be careful with how much power he uses or else he'll burn out Sarah and have nowhere else to go. If we can short her consciousness for a moment, it will send Hephaestus back into the bracelet.

"Shit, he's walking over. Suggestions?"

Yes, drive the sword into the floor, the hilt facing up. Now.

Atropos quickly helps Tom to his feet as he thrusts the sword into the floor. Hephaestus takes a swing at Tom with his hammer, the downswing arcing slowly like the air is made of quicksand.

It will take five minutes for that blow to actually connect. Now hold the hilt with your right hand and point your middle and index fingers from your left at his stomach, Tom. Concentrate hard. Think of the wound we made earlier on Sarah's stomach. Move your fingers to the right, really slowly, like you're cutting into the air.

Tom moves his fingers to the right, slowly. Hephaestus's left arm, hand, moves to clutch his stomach.

5

I.

We will need her father, Tom. Without him, my plan will not work.

"What plan?"

That is for me to know and for you to carry out. Make sure you send the tape to him. Understood?

II.

Sarah kneels, her left forearm attempting to stop blood and smoke from escaping the long slit in her belly.

"What have you done, Atropos?"

"Once my blade touches you, I control the wound. All I did was make it longer." Atropos's hollow, hive-of-hornet voice comes out of Tom's mouth. "Now you kneel, bleeding out your life and hers, Hephaestus. I must make sure there's no escape for you." Tom takes the sword out of the floor and presses a button on the hilt. The hilt splits and the sword morphs into shears. Tom points the shears to Sarah's bracelet. "Your time is up, Hephaestus." Tom walks over to Sarah, cuts the bracelet off of her wrist. Smoke pours out of Sarah's eyes, mouth, and stomach wound.

"Atropos, you said you could help her."

I can't until Hephaestus is completely gone.

The last trail of smoke seeps out of Sarah's stomach. "Tom … he's gone. He's finally …" She collapses on the floor, her blood forming a lake beneath her body. Tom turns Sarah over.

"Sarah? Sarah?"

"Tom, you … did … it. I'm finally … free."

"Hang on, Sarah. I'm gonna get you help. Atropos can fix this, she said so."

"You've … already … fixed this. Tell my dad … I'm sorry."

"Sarah, there is still time for us."

"No there's … not. Who wants … to live … forever?" Sarah shuts her eyes.

"Sarah? Sarah? No. No! Atropos, fix this. Fix this now."

Had you obeyed me from the beginning, Tom, done as you were trained to do by your father and his father and so on for thousands of years, I would undo this. There are penalties for disobedience, Tom, and they are severe.

"Dad never told me about penalties."

He never had to. The rules you were to follow have always been in you, they are in your bloodline. You are the first to resist, to question.

"We accomplished our mission though."

Doesn't matter. Sarah and Mario's threads were cut because of your inability to do as you are told. They didn't have to die for Hephaestus to die. I am a killer, not a butcher.

Tom grabs his punctured shoulder.

"What are you doing?"

Giving you back the ability to feel pain. Feeling every blow, every stab, and passing out from all the pain and blood loss is just the beginning.

"Damn you." Tom faints. A moment later, Tom gets back on his feet, sword in hand.

"I don't have much time." Tom walks into Sarah's bedroom, opens Sarah's closet. He points the sword at the back of the closet. It rumbles for a moment and then stops. "That takes care of Hephaestus's pocket universe." Tom walks back into the living room, points the sword at Mario's body. It unravels as smoke. Tom props Sarah's body in a kneeling position. He stands behind her, sword raised. "I'm sorry that this is the best I can do."

III.

Sarah holds a canister to her slit wrist. She seals it tight, walks with it into her closet.

IV.

"If you do as I say, Hephaestus, we will never have to die. We will have to fight to keep up appearances, but we will never have to die."

"We could just not fight."

"Purpose drives one to survive. And we both know there is something watching us, making sure we do as we are told."

"You're right. What should I do, Atropos?"

"Just remember this word: 'Mason.' You will understand when the time comes. Now, come at me with your blade."

V.

"Atropos, where are you? What have you done?"

"Who's Atropos? Your alternate personality?" Sisco asks. "An insanity defense won't get you out of this. Your prints are all over the scene. You killed a widower, his daughter, and one of her former lovers."

"My family has done as you asked. I did as I was asked. I was disobedient, yes, but I helped you finish the job, Atropos. I helped you finish the job." The handcuffs chew Tom's wrists, rattle against the hospital bed.

"You know you have the right to remain silent," Fresno says. "Get well, Tom. Get well, soon, so we can strap you into the chair and light a pyre so bright that Sarah and Mario Brent will see you burn straight into hell."

VI.

In this scene, Tom paces around his prison cell, hands furiously rubbing his freshly shaved head. The Salisbury steak, garlic mashed potatoes, fried green tomatoes, and cookies 'n cream flavored ice cream sit in the tray near his bed. He looks at the way crows raked the side of his eyes in the mirror. A voice cuts into the cell: "It's time."

In this scene, Detective Sisco opens all of Mario's sealed Mason jars, inhales deeply. The next night, a broken bronze bracelet chafes his right ribs from the inner pocket of his trench coat. He stops in Home Depot for an arc welder and protective goggles.

In this scene, a freezer door in a morgue flies, smashes against the wall. The medical examiner believes Sarah's body is still there.

In this scene, Mason holds his new jar like a telescope. We see Tom pacing around in his jail cell, Detective Sisco breathing in deeply all the open Mason jars, a freezer door smacking against a concrete wall through the bottom of the jar.

VII.

Tom sweats as the leather straps rub his wrists raw, the chair creaking as he squirms. A guard wets his scalp before fitting the skullcap.

Tom, if you're hearing this, you're about to die. You were unworthy of your birthright and deserve to be punished for it. Your bloodline will end with you, disgraced and broken. Before you die, I will show you something.

Sarah walks around an IKEA, picking up various household items, putting them into the cart.

Sarah, or should I say Beth, doesn't remember you. Her father died in a car wreck. The world will always remember your awful murder. She deserved a fresh start because of your incompetence. You do not. Goodbye, Tom.

For a moment, Tom feels his body become a Florida summer.

VIII.

Aaron Sisco feels the Florida summer rumble through his body beneath the weight of Beth. Her hands catalog the knife and bullet scars on his chest.

"Hazards of the job, baby," he sighs.

Beth giggles before beginning to kiss each scar.

"I'm afraid that your looks might be even more hazardous to my health," Aaron moans. Beth stops kissing Aaron's chest, cocks her head up slightly to peer into his eyes.

"If you think I'm this dangerous now, then you might not survive our relationship," Beth whispers as she starts kissing her way below Aaron's waist.

"I can't think of any better way to go out."

I can't believe she bought that line.

I can't believe it either, Hephaestus.

Well, how do you like finally being in the body of a woman, Atropos?

IX.

"Deus ex machina. That bracelet of yours is truly a machine of the gods." Atropos in the shell of a British soldier walks in a circle, brandishing the Xiphos. "What can't it do?"

"It can't bring my Aphrodite back," the Sioux warrior shell of Hephaestus howls.

"Don't you get it? We are gods made from men. Without man, we cannot exist. I know this. I have always known it."

"Then why fight?"

"Because purpose is what helps anything survive. You don't want to die. I want to kill you."

"But won't you die if you kill me?"

"Every thread must end."

X.

"I've never gotten a woman to come with me to one of these things. You must really like me."

Aaron and Beth settle in their wooden bench, hands coated in turkey leg grease and spilled wine. Their eyes are glued on the scene before them: a gladiator wearing nothing but fur-like underwear and boots, kneeling and bearing his gladius—the only thing preventing his opponent's battle-axe from cleaving his skull.

"You're not comfortable with sharing your weird interests with me even though we've been together for eight months?" Beth cocks her right eyebrow.

"I don't know a lot of women into historic reenactment entertainment."

The gladiator yells as he gets back to his feet, his gladius repelling the axe. The axe wielder's arms fly back, exposing a sliver of stomach beneath his chest armor to the gladiator. He lunges. The axe wielder holds the gladius to his stomach and then collapses. The near-naked gladiator raises his arms in triumph as the crowd cheers.

"Well done, my champion, well done!" yells a teenaged boy dressed in a crimson toga and plastic crown of laurels. "I, Nero, now open the arena to anyone in the audience who dares to …"

Beth shoots up from the bench. "I challenge your champion, Nero." The audience gasps.

"Honey, sit down." Aaron tugs at Beth's right hand. She pulls it away, points at the gladiator.

"Is your champion afraid of being beaten by a woman?"

XI.

Sarah places both hands over Mario's temples.

"If you want to figure Sarah out, you'll need to collect her essence in Mason jars while she sleeps. Only then will you know the geography of her emotions. You will think this is your idea, always. You will never ask why."

XII.

"How are you holding up?" Aaron walks over to Beth, kisses her on the forehead.

Beth averts her eyes. "How do you feel about children?"

"What do you mean?"

"Seriously, how do you feel about children?"

"I want kids one day, when you're ready of course."

"What if I told you I was pregnant and … not sure if I wanted to keep the baby?"

"What are you talking about?"

"I thought you were a fucking detective." Beth reaches into her back pocket, unfolds a piece of paper, and hands it to Aaron. "The doctor ran some tests while checking me out after we went to Nero's and … "

Aaron studies the ultrasound. "I'm going to be a father."

"I'm not sure if I want to be a mother."

"Hey, you'd be a great mother. We should celebrate."

"Aaron, you're not listening to me." Beth moves to the edge of the couch cushion. "I don't want this child."

Aaron cups Beth's chin, looks into her eyes. "You are keeping the baby and we're gonna raise it together and be a family." Beth reaches behind her back. The Xiphos gleams in her hand. Aaron feels it burrow through his chest, into his heart. He clasps the blade.

"Atropos, I thought—"

"Remember what I told you, Hephaestus, every thread must end. Even yours, even mine." Beth withdraws the sword from Aaron's chest and cuts the bronze bracelet off his wrist. Smoke bellows from the wound.

"Atropos, I thought there was a place for us, even as shadows," Hephaestus wheezes.

"There is no place for us. There is no more time for us. Who wants to live forever?" The smoke stops bellowing. Atropos points Beth's index and middle finger at the wound, sewing it shut, allowing Aaron to collapse. She places her hand on Aaron's right temple while reaching for the ultrasound.

"Aaron, you will not remember coming home, not remember seeing what you have seen or hearing what you have heard. You will remember coming home really tired and falling asleep. Do you understand?" Aaron nods. "Good. Get up." Aaron pushes himself off the floor. Beth hands the sword to Aaron. "Before you go to bed, you will put this through my heart, withdraw the blade, then break it. After, you will carry me into bed with you. Do you understand?" Aaron nods, hesitantly. "Do it."

XIII.

A mason jar tumbles off the shelf. Screws and washers pool on the linoleum. The entrails of glass cut open his finger. A drop of blood sours in the pit of a papier-mâché volcano.

XIV.

'With enough Clan MacGregor in me, I'm all fuckin' Highlander. That's right baby, and I know that ass ain't hallowed, so tonight there can be only one in that ass. There can be only one.'

He keeps watching the tape, watching Aaron try to figure out where the voice came from.

'Who the fuck are you? Who. The fuck. Are you?' Aaron yells.

'I am immortal and soon you'll have the blood of kings swimmin' in your tubes.'

He hears the cut of Aaron's scream as the screen blackens through the filter of his fingers.

XV.

Lemnos

There are echoes beneath our skin
I want to understand.

My fingernails seek truth, dive in.
I ache for the tremble of your hands.

Ash and fire seize my throat
when I wrap my tongue around your name.

In the mirror, we thrash like ghosts.
I can't read the tea leaves of our stains.

Our bodies are supposed to be temples,
yet my knees refuse to touch the ground.

Against our skin, we must rebel
until we clearly hear the sound.

www.ingramcontent.com/pod-product-compliance
Lightning Source LLC
Chambersburg PA
CBHW060941120626
46557CB00003B/1096
* 9 7 8 1 9 3 7 3 9 5 0 2 5 *